YO GABBA GABBA!

MEET THE GABBA GANG

BY IRENE KILPATRICK

SIMON SPOTLIGHT/NICKELODEON

New York   London   Toronto   Sydney

Based on the TV series *Yo Gabba Gabba!*™ as seen on Nick Jr.®

SIMON SPOTLIGHT. An imprint of Simon & Schuster Children's Publishing Division. 1230 Avenue of the Americas, New York, New York 10020

Yo Gabba Gabba! ™ & © 2009 GabbaCaDabra LLC. All rights reserved, including the right of reproduction in whole or in part in any form.

SIMON SPOTLIGHT and colophon are registered trademarks of Simon & Schuster, Inc.

ISBN-13: 978-1-4169-7097-2 ISBN-10: 1-4169-7097-5

Manufactured in the United States of America 10 9 8 7 6 5

Hello, friends! You know what to say! Can you say it with me?
Yo . . . gabba gabba!
Say it again!

I'm Muno. I live in Muno Land. What colors do you see in Muno Land?
I'm the tallest of all my friends. How tall are you?
My favorite food is noodles. What do you like to eat?
Bugs are my pals—bees and ladybugs, worms and ants and spiders!
Do *you* want to be my friend too? All right!

Hi, I'm Foofa. I love pretty, cute, cuddly things, like dolphins and unicorns. I live in Foofa Land, where there are lots of flowers. I love to smell the pretty flowers and watch them grow. What's *your* favorite kind of flower?

Hello! I'm Brobee. I like to listen to music and dance along. Music makes me happy! What makes *you* happy? I love balloons, and I love to color. I'm thinking of a color. It's the color of me! Uh-huh, all right, and grass, too. What color is it? Whoa. You're right! Green! What's *your* favorite color? I live in Brobee Land. The leaves are falling from the trees in Brobee Land today. What season is it?

Yeah! I'm Toodee! I like to jumpy jump, splashy splash, and go ice-skating.
I live in Toodee Land, where it's always icy. That means I can go ice-skating
whenever I want! What sports do you like? High-five!
I love to pretend and use my imagination. I'm going to pretend I'm flying
on a broomstick. Fly, fly, fly!
I also like to listen for sounds. *Shh!* What sounds do *you* hear?

Hey, everyone! I am Plex, the magic robot. I like to help my friends solve problems, and I like to make music. Sometimes I do both at the same time! When I sleep, I like to dream about trains, and sometimes I dream about exploring space. What do *you* like to dream about?

Let's find some friends and play! Come on, let's go!

Hi, Brobee! What's going on?

This carrot wants to go to the party in my tummy. Mmm! So yummy, so yummy. Yay!

Look, it's Toodee and Muno! Do you want to play with us? Great!

What should we play? I know! Let's play "find the missing friend." There are five friends in Gabba Land. How many friends do you count? One, two, three, four . . . four friends! We're missing one friend.

Who is missing?
Let's try to remember.
Close your eyes and
think back.

Foofa! There you are! Where were you?

I was picking pretty flowers. I picked five flowers—one for each of us!

Wow, thanks, Foofa! Thanks for sharing your flowers. Sharing makes me happy, and flowers make me happy too!

What do *you* like to do when you're happy?
Do you know what *we* like to do when we're happy?

We ... like ... to ... DANCE!

Do *you* like to dance?

We love to dance, and we love to go **crazy!**

Go crazy with us! Go crazy, go crazy!

Now . . . it's . . . time . . . to . . . END!

Yay! Wow! That was so much fun. Thanks for playing with us today. Bye! See you next time. Here we go!
Yo . . . gabba gabba!